THE ROAD AHEAD

Also edited by Zachary Seager

Leaving Home

Falling in Love

Living Peacefully

Finding Happiness

Paris: A Literary Anthology

Our Place in Nature

Sleepily Ever After

The Art of Solitude

THE ROAD AHEAD

Selection, introduction and
arrangement by
ZACHARY SEAGER

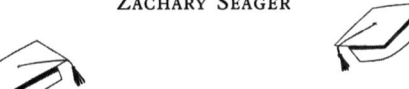

MACMILLAN COLLECTOR'S LIBRARY

First published 2026 by Macmillan Collector's Library
an imprint of Pan Macmillan
The Smithson, 6 Briset Street, London EC1M 5NR
EU representative: Macmillan Publishers Ireland Ltd, 1st Floor,
The Liffey Trust Centre, 117–126 Sheriff Street Upper,
Dublin 1 D01 YC43
Associated companies throughout the world

ISBN 978-1-0350-6947-7

Introduction copyright © Zachary Seager 2026
Selection and arrangement copyright © Macmillan Publishers International Ltd 2026

The Permissions Acknowledgements on p. 147 constitute
an extension of this copyright page.

All rights reserved. No part of this publication may be reproduced, stored in a retrieval system, or transmitted, in any form, or by any means (including, without limitation, electronic, mechanical, photocopying, recording or otherwise) without the prior written permission of the publisher.

Pan Macmillan does not have any control over, or any responsibility for, any author or third-party websites (including, without limitation, URLs, emails and QR codes) referred to in or on this book.

1 3 5 7 9 8 6 4 2

A CIP catalogue record for this book is available from the British Library.

Illustrations © Sinead Hayward 2026

Cover and endpaper design: Daisy Bates, Pan Macmillan Art Department
Typeset by SRM (UK)
Printed and bound in China by Imago

This book is sold subject to the condition that it shall not, by way of trade or otherwise, be lent, hired out, or otherwise circulated without the publisher's prior consent in any form of binding or cover other than that in which it is published and without a similar condition including this condition being imposed on the subsequent purchaser. The publisher does not authorize the use or reproduction of any part of this book in any manner for the purpose of training artificial intelligence technologies or systems. The publisher expressly reserves this book from the Text and Data Mining exception in accordance with Article 4(3) of the European Union Digital Single Market Directive 2019/790.

Visit **www.panmacmillan.com** to read more
about all our books and to buy them.

Contents

Introduction ix

HOPE

Hope is the thing with feathers *Emily Dickinson* 3

from Espoir en Dieu *Victor Hugo* 4

from The Golden Gems of Life *S. C. Ferguson and E. A. Allen* 5

from A New Sense of Direction *Martin Luther King* 6

from Julius Caesar *William Shakespeare* 7

The Hare and the Tortoise *Jean de La Fontaine* 8

from War and Peace *Leo Tolstoy* 10

from Pro Plancio *Marcus Tullius Cicero* 11

The Winds of Fate *Ella Wheeler Wilcox* 12

Who Has Seen the Wind? *Christina Rossetti* 13

from Hawthorne and His Mosses *Herman Melville* 14

from King John *William Shakespeare* 15

from Barnaby Rudge *Charles Dickens* 16

from Oldtown Folks *Harriet Beecher Stowe* 17

SEEK

The Road Not Taken *Robert Frost* 21

from Walden *Henry David Thoreau* 23

The Stag at the Pool *Aesop* 24

from The Prophet *Kahlil Gibran* 25

Good Timber *Douglas Malloch* 27

from The Characters *Jean de La Bruyère* 29

from A Farewell to Arms *Ernest Hemingway* 30

I dwell in Possibility *Emily Dickinson* 31

from Some Social Remedies *Leo Tolstoy* 32

If— *Rudyard Kipling* 33

from Of Pedantry *Michel de Montaigne* 36

from Meditations *Marcus Aurelius* 37

from Character Building *Booker T. Washington* 38

from For Katrina's Sundial *Henry Van Dyke* 42

from Citizenship in a Republic *Theodore Roosevelt* 43

Invictus *William Ernest Henley* 46

STRIVE

from Of Experience *Michel de Montaigne* 49

from As a Man Thinketh *James Allen* 50

from The Prophet *Kahlil Gibran* 53

from Adam Bede *George Eliot* 55

from War and Peace *Leo Tolstoy* 56

from The Enchiridion *Epictetus* 57

from Walden *Henry David Thoreau* 59

from What I Think and Feel at 25 *F. Scott Fitzgerald* 62

from The Life of Petrarch by S. Dobson *Petrarch* 64

As You Go Through Life *Ella Wheeler Wilcox* 66

from Meditations *Marcus Aurelius* 68

from Ginger Snaps *Fanny Fern* 69

Courage *Ella Fuller Maitland* 72

from Leaves of Grass *Walt Whitman* 73

The Golden Windows *Laura E. Richards* 74

FIND

from Eleanora *Edgar Allan Poe* 81

Barter *Sara Teasdale* 82

from Marriage and Love *Emma Goldman* 83

from What Is to Be Done? *Leo Tolstoy* 84

If I can stop one heart from breaking *Emily Dickinson* 85

Letter to Sara Hennell *George Eliot* 86

Letter to Menoeceus *Epicurus* 88

from Emma *Jane Austen* 90

from Friendship *Ralph Waldo Emerson* 91

from On the Happy Life *Lucius Annaeus Seneca* 95

I Wandered Lonely as a Cloud *William Wordsworth* 97

Letter to W. S. Williams *Charlotte Brontë* 99

from Fashions in Literature *Charles Dudley Warner* 100

A Psalm of Life *Henry Wadsworth Longfellow* 101

Who Owns the Mountains? *Henry Van Dyke* 103

FLOURISH

Your World *Georgia Douglas Johnson* 113

Advice to Youth *Mark Twain* 114

The Traveller and His Dog *Aesop* 120

from Tremendous Trifles *G. K. Chesterton* 121

from Leaves of Grass *Walt Whitman* 122

from A Plea for Captain John Brown *Henry David Thoreau* 126

from The Living Thoughts of Voltaire by André Maurois *Voltaire* 127

The Crow and the Pitcher *Aesop* 128

Try, Try Again *T. H. Palmer* 129

from The Life of Samuel Johnson *James Boswell* 131

Desiderata *Max Ehrmann* 132

from Mark Twain's Notebook *Mark Twain* 135

Three Questions *Leo Tolstoy* 136

Index of Poets and Authors 144

Permissions Acknowledgements 147

Introduction
Zachary Seager

After years spent absorbed by one goal, one task, and dedicated to one end; after countless hours of deep study and conscious learning; after the late nights and early mornings during which, bleary-eyed, you sacrificed sleep to a waking dream; after the laughing fits in the library and the quick tears before exams; after the exhilarating evenings trekking with friends to the next party where, you were sure of it, someone was already waiting for you, the stranger that would really matter; after the long months between summers and the summers that, sometimes, seemed to meander on for ever; after all that, the day has come: it's over; you've graduated.

First comes the ecstasy, the deserved celebration. The struggle, the effort, the strain: all worth it. Then, after a pause, a new confusion starts to settle. What next? What now?

That is where this anthology comes in. The road ahead, with luck, is long. And marked throughout by decisions great and grave. Some of those choices will be simple, self-evident. Others will prove perplexing. Still others will become clear only with hindsight and years later, a fork in the track which, at the time, felt like a mere curve in an otherwise open, unbending path.

How can we recognize such moments, we who wander without a map? Now that we've crossed a key bridge on the journey – graduation – what should we seek next? For what should we strive? What will we find? And how, for what awaits, can we keep up our courage, our determination to go on?

For these questions and more, *The Road Ahead* is here to help. The five sections of this anthology are dedicated to the challenges still to come – hoping, seeking, striving, finding. And, of course, flourishing.

First, it will help you hope. From Emily Dickinson to Christina Rossetti and Leo Tolstoy, some of the most insightful writers we've ever known will guide your vision and swell your dreams.

Then, through the proven wisdom of great poets and past sages such as Marcus Aurelius,

Robert Frost and Michel de Montaigne, it will help you seek, counselling you in pursuit of the next bright horizon.

After that, it will help you to strive, to fight and not to yield. Despite the fear and the uncertainty and the setbacks and the pain, major authors like George Eliot, F. Scott Fitzgerald and Henry David Thoreau will push you on, buoy you up and fortify you for the voyage.

Next, classic figures like Jane Austen, Charlotte Brontë and Epicurus will help you find. Find what? Precisely that which you were seeking – even if you didn't know it, even if what you were searching for comes suddenly as a surprise.

And finally, great thinkers and creative giants like Voltaire, Mark Twain and Walt Whitman will help you flourish, wherever your path has led.

Taken together, this anthology will show you that, while today might feel like an ending, it's really a new beginning – the start of *The Road Ahead*.

HOPE

Hope is the thing with feathers

Hope is the thing with feathers
That perches in the soul,
And sings the tune without the words,
And never stops at all,

And sweetest in the gale is heard;
And sore must be the storm
That could abash the little bird
That kept so many warm.

I've heard it in the chillest land,
And on the strangest sea;
Yet, never, in extremity,
It asked a crumb of me.

Emily Dickinson

from Espoir en Dieu

Hope, child, to-morrow hope, and then again to-morrow,
> And then to-morrow still! Trust in a future day.

Hope, and each morn the skies new light from dawn shall borrow;
> As God is there to bless, let us be there to pray.

Victor Hugo

from The Golden Gems of Life

True hope is based on the energy of character.

    A strong mind always hopes, and has always cause to hope, because it knows the mutability of human affairs and how slight a circumstance may change the whole course of events. Such a spirit, too, rests upon itself; it is not confined to partial views or to one particular object. And if at last all should be lost, it has saved itself its own integrity and wealth.

S. C. Ferguson and E. A. Allen

from A New Sense of Direction

In our individual lives we all too often distill our frustrations into an essence of bitterness or drown ourselves in the deep waters of self-pity or adopt a fatalistic philosophy that whatever happens must happen, that all events are determined by necessity. These reactions poison the soul and scar the personality. The only healthy answer is one's honest recognition of disappointment even as he clings to fragments of hope, the acceptance of finite disappointment while clinging to infinite hope.

Martin Luther King

from Julius Caesar

And we must take the current when it serves,
Or lose our ventures.

William Shakespeare

The Hare and the Tortoise

Rushing is useless; one has to leave on time. To such
Truth witness is given by the Tortoise and the Hare.
"Let's make a bet," the former once said, "that you won't touch
That line as soon as I." "As soon? Are you all there,
>   Neighbor?" said the rapid beast.
>   "You need a purge: four grains at least
>   Of hellebore, you're now so far gone."
>   "All there or not, the bet's still on."
>   So it was done; the wagers of the two
>   Were placed at the finish, in view.
>   It doesn't matter what was down at stake,
>   Nor who was the judge that they got.

Our Hare had, at most, four steps or so to take.
I mean the kind he takes when, on the verge of being caught,
He outruns dogs sent to the calends for their pains,
>   Making them run all over the plains.

Having, I say, time to spare, sleep, browse around,
>	Listen to where the wind was bound,
He let the Tortoise leave the starting place
>	In stately steps, wide-spaced.
Straining, she commenced the race:
>	Going slow was how she made haste.
He, meanwhile, thought such a win derogatory,
>	Judged the bet to be devoid of glory,
>	Believed his honor was all based
On leaving late. He browsed, lolled like a king,
>	Amused himself with everything
>	But the bet. When at last he took a look,
Saw that she'd almost arrived at the end of the course,
He shot off like a bolt. But all of the leaps he took
Were in vain; the Tortoise was first perforce.
"Well, now!" she cried out to him. "Was I wrong?
>	What good is all your speed to you?
>	The winner is me! And how would you do
>	If you also carried a house along?"

Jean de La Fontaine

from War and Peace

'Everything comes in time for him who knows how to wait.'

Leo Tolstoy

from Pro Plancio

A thankful heart is not only the greatest virtue,
but the parent of all the other virtues.

Marcus Tullius Cicero

The Winds of Fate

One ship drives east and another drives west,
    With the self-same winds that blow,
    'Tis the set of the sails
    And not the gales
That tell them the way to go.

Like the winds of the sea are the winds of fate,
As we voyage along through life,
    'Tis the set of the soul
    That decides its goal
And not the calm or the strife.

Ella Wheeler Wilcox

Who Has Seen the Wind?

Who has seen the wind?
    Neither I nor you:
But when the leaves hang trembling
    The wind is passing through.
Who has seen the wind?
    Neither you nor I:
But when the trees bow down their heads
    The wind is passing by.

Christina Rossetti

from Hawthorne and His Mosses

But it is better to fail in originality, than to succeed in imitation. He who has never failed somewhere, that man cannot be great. Failure is the true test of greatness. And if it be said, that continual success is a proof that a man wisely knows his powers,—it is only to be added, that, in that case, he knows them to be small.

Herman Melville

from King John

But wherefore do you droop? Why look so sad?
Be great in fact, as you have been in thought;
Let not the world see fear and sad distrust.
Govern the motion of a kingly eye;
Be stirring as the time; be fire with fire;
Threaten the threatener, and outface the brow,
Of bragging horror; so shall inferior eyes,
That borrow their behaviors from the great,
Grow great by your example; and put on
The dauntless spirit of resolution.

William Shakespeare

from Barnaby Rudge

It is a poor heart that never rejoices.

Charles Dickens

from Oldtown Folks

"When you get into a tight place, and everything goes against you, till it seems as if you couldn't hold on a minute longer, *never give up then*, for that's just the place and time that the tide'll turn."

Harriet Beecher Stowe

SEEK

The Road Not Taken

Two roads diverged in a yellow wood,
And sorry I could not travel both
And be one traveler, long I stood
And looked down one as far as I could
To where it bent in the undergrowth;

Then took the other, as just as fair,
And having perhaps the better claim,
Because it was grassy and wanted wear;
Though as for that the passing there
Had worn them really about the same,

And both that morning equally lay
In leaves no step had trodden black.
Oh, I kept the first for another day!
Yet knowing how way leads on to way,
I doubted if I should ever come back.

I shall be telling this with a sigh
Somewhere ages and ages hence:
Two roads diverged in a wood, and I—
I took the one less traveled by,
And that has made all the difference.

Robert Frost

from Walden

I learned this, at least, by my experiment; that if one advances confidently in the direction of his dreams, and endeavors to live the life which he has imagined, he will meet with a success unexpected in common hours. He will put some things behind, will pass an invisible boundary; new, universal, and more liberal laws will begin to establish themselves around and within him; or the old laws be expanded, and interpreted in his favor in a more liberal sense, and he will live with the license of a higher order of beings. In proportion as he simplifies his life, the laws of the universe will appear less complex, and solitude will not be solitude, nor poverty poverty, nor weakness weakness. If you have built castles in the air, your work need not be lost; that is where they should be. Now put the foundations under them.

Henry David Thoreau

The Stag at the Pool

A Stag overpowered by heat came to a spring to drink. Seeing his own shadow reflected in the water, he greatly admired the size and variety of his horns, but felt angry with himself for having such slender and weak feet. While he was thus contemplating himself, a Lion appeared at the pool and crouched to spring upon him. The Stag immediately betook himself to flight: and exerting his utmost speed, as long as the plain was smooth and open, kept himself with ease at a safe distance from the Lion. But entering a wood he became entangled by his horns: and the Lion quickly came up with him and caught him. When too late he thus reproached himself: "Woe is me! How have I deceived myself! These feet which would have saved me I despised, and I gloried in these antlers which have proved my destruction."

What is most truly valuable is often underrated.

Aesop

from The Prophet

And what is it to work with love?

It is to weave the cloth with threads drawn from your heart, even as if your beloved were to wear that cloth.

It is to build a house with affection, even as if your beloved were to dwell in that house.

It is to sow seeds with tenderness and reap the harvest with joy, even as if your beloved were to eat the fruit.

It is to charge all things you fashion with a breath of your own spirit,

And to know that all the blessed dead are standing about you and watching.

Often have I heard you say, as if speaking in sleep, "He who works in marble, and finds the shape of his own soul in the stone, is nobler than he who ploughs the soil.

And he who seizes the rainbow to lay it on a cloth in the likeness of man, is more than he who makes the sandals for our feet."

But I say, not in sleep but in the over-wakefulness of noontide, that the wind speaks not more sweetly to the giant oaks than to the least of all the blades of grass;

And he alone is great who turns the voice of the wind into a song made sweeter by his own loving.

Work is love made visible.

And if you cannot work with love but only with distaste, it is better that you should leave your work and sit at the gate of the temple and take alms of those who work with joy.

For if you bake bread with indifference, you bake a bitter bread that feeds but half man's hunger.

And if you grudge the crushing of the grapes, your grudge distils a poison in the wine.

And if you sing though as angels, and love not the singing, you muffle man's ears to the voices of the day and the voices of the night.

Kahlil Gibran

Good Timber

The tree that never had to fight
For sun and sky and air and light,
That stood out in the open plain,
Always got its share of rain,
Never became a forest king,
But lived and died a scrubby thing.
The man who never had to toil,
Who never had to win his share,
Never became a manly man
Of sun and sky and light and air,
But lived and died as he began.
Good timber does not grow in ease;
The stronger wind, the rougher trees.
The farther sky, the greater length;
The more the storm, the more the strength;
By sun and cold, by rain and snows,
In tree or man good timber grows.
Where thickest stands the forest growth
We find the patriarchs of both,

And they hold converse with the stars
Whose broken branches show their scars
Of many winds and much of strife—
This is the common law of life.

Douglas Malloch

from The Characters

There exist some evils so terrible and some misfortunes so horrible that we dare not think of them, whilst their very aspect makes us shudder; but if they happen to fall on us, we find ourselves stronger than we imagined; we grapple with our ill luck, and behave better than we expected we should.

Jean de La Bruyère

from A Farewell to Arms

The world breaks every one and afterward many are strong at the broken places.

Ernest Hemingway

I dwell in Possibility

I dwell in Possibility,
A fairer house than Prose,
More numerous of windows,
Superior of doors.

Of chambers, as the cedars —
Impregnable of eye;
And for an everlasting roof
The gables of the sky.

Of visitors — the fairest —
For occupation — this —
The spreading wide my narrow hands
To gather Paradise.

Emily Dickinson

from Some Social Remedies

There can be only one permanent revolution—a moral one; the regeneration of the inner man.

How is this revolution to take place? Nobody knows how it will take place in humanity, but every man feels it clearly in himself. And yet in our world everybody thinks of changing humanity, and nobody thinks of changing himself.

Leo Tolstoy

If—

If you can keep your head when all about you
    Are losing theirs and blaming it on you;
If you can trust yourself when all men doubt you,
    But make allowance for their doubting too:
If you can wait and not be tired by waiting,
    Or being lied about, don't deal in lies,
Or being hated don't give way to hating,
    And yet don't look too good, nor talk too wise;

If you can dream — and not make dreams your master;
    If you can think — and not make thoughts your aim,
If you can meet with Triumph and Disaster
    And treat those two impostors just the same:
If you can bear to hear the truth you've spoken
    Twisted by knaves to make a trap for fools,

Or watch the things you gave your life to, broken,
>   And stoop and build 'em up with worn-out tools;

If you can make one heap of all your winnings
>   And risk it on one turn of pitch-and-toss,
And lose, and start again at your beginnings
>   And never breathe a word about your loss:

If you can force your heart and nerve and sinew
>   To serve your turn long after they are gone,
And so hold on when there is nothing in you
>   Except the Will which says to them: 'Hold on!'

If you can talk with crowds and keep your virtue,
>   Or walk with Kings — nor lose the common touch,

If neither foes nor loving friends can hurt you,
> If all men count with you, but none too much:

If you can fill the unforgiving minute
> With sixty seconds' worth of distance run,

Yours is the Earth and everything that's in it,
> And — which is more — you'll be a Man, my son!

Rudyard Kipling

from Of Pedantry

for though we could become learned by other men's learning, a man can never be wise but by his own wisdom:—

Michel de Montaigne

from Meditations

If it is not right, do not do it: if it is not true, do not say it.

Marcus Aurelius

from Character Building

I want you to go out from this institution so trained and so developed that you will be constantly looking for the bright, encouraging and beautiful things in life. It is the weak individual, as a rule, who is constantly calling attention to the other side—to the dark and discouraging things of life. When you go into your class-rooms, I repeat, try to forget and overlook any weak points that you may think you see. Remember, and dwell upon, the consideration that has been given to the lesson, the faithfulness with which it was prepared, and the earnestness with which it is presented. Try to recall and to remember every good thing and every encouraging thing which has come under your observation, whether it has been in the class-room, or in the shop, or in the field. No matter where you are, seize hold on the encouraging things with which you come in contact.

In connection with the personality of their teachers, it is very unfortunate for students to form a habit of continually finding fault, of criticising, of seeing nothing but what the student may think are weak points. Try to get into a frame of mind where you will be constantly seeing and calling attention to the strong and beautiful things which you observe in the life and work of your teachers. Grow into the habit of talking about the bright side of life. When you meet a fellow student, a teacher, or anybody, or when you write letters home, get into the habit of calling attention to the bright things of life that you have seen, the things that are beautiful, the things that are charming. Just in proportion as you do this, you will find that you will not only influence yourself in the right direction, but that you will also influence others that way. It is a very bad habit to get into, that of being continually moody and discouraged, and of making the atmosphere uncomfortable for everybody who comes within ten feet of you. There are some people who are so constantly looking on the dark side of life that they cannot see anything but that side. Everything that comes from their mouths is unpleasant, about this thing and that thing, and they make the whole atmosphere around them unpleasant for themselves and for everybody with whom they come in contact. Such persons are surely undesirable. Why, I have seen people coming up the road who caused me to feel like wanting to cross over on to the other side of the way so as not to meet them. I didn't want to hear their tales of misery and woe. I had heard those tales so many times that I didn't want to get into the atmosphere of the people who told them.

It is often very easy to influence others in the wrong direction, and to grow into such a moody fault-finding disposition that one not only is miserable and unhappy himself, but makes every one with whom he comes in contact miserable and unhappy. The persons who live constantly in a fault-finding atmosphere, who see only the dark side of life, become negative characters. They are the people who never go forward. They never suggest a line of activity. They live simply on the negative side of life. Now, as students, you cannot afford to grow in that way. We want to send each one of you out from here, not as a negative force, but as a strong, positive, helpful force in the world. You will not accomplish the task which we expect of you if you go with a moody, discouraged, fault-finding disposition. To do the most that lies in you, you must go with a heart and head full of hope and faith in the world, believing that there is work for you to do, believing that you are the person to accomplish that work, and the one who is going to accomplish it.

In nine cases out of ten, the person who cultivates the habit of looking on the dark side of life is the little person, the miserable person, the one who is weak in mind, heart and purpose. On the other hand, the person who cultivates the habit of looking on the bright side of life, and who calls attention to the beautiful and encouraging things in life is, in nine cases out of ten, the strong individual, the one to whom the world goes for intelligent advice and support. I am trying to get you to see, as students, the best things in life. Do not be satisfied with second-hand or third-hand things in life. Do not be satisfied until you have put yourselves into that atmosphere where you can seize and hold on to the very highest and most beautiful things that can be got out of life.

Booker T. Washington

from For Katrina's Sundial

    Time is
Too Slow for those who Wait,
Too Swift for those who Fear,
Too Long for those who Grieve,
Too Short for those who Rejoice;
    But for those who Love,
        Time is not.

Henry Van Dyke

from Citizenship in a Republic

The poorest way to face life is to face it with a sneer. There are many men who feel a kind of twisted pride in cynicism; there are many who confine themselves to criticism of the way others do what they themselves dare not even attempt. There is no more unhealthy being, no man less worthy of respect, than he who either really holds, or feigns to hold, an attitude of sneering disbelief toward all that is great and lofty, whether in achievement or in that noble effort which, even if it fails, comes second to achievement. A cynical habit of thought and speech, a readiness to criticise work which the critic himself never tries to perform, an intellectual aloofness which will not accept contact with life's realities—all these are marks, not, as the possessor would fain think, of superiority, but of weakness. They mark the men unfit to bear their part manfully in the stern strife of living, who seek, in the affectation of contempt for the achievements of others, to hide from others and from themselves their own weakness. The rôle is easy; there is none easier, save only the rôle of the man who sneers alike at both criticism and performance.

It is not the critic who counts; not the man who points out how the strong man stumbles, or where the doer of deeds could have done them better. The credit belongs to the man who is actually in the arena, whose face is marred by dust and sweat and blood; who strives valiantly; who errs, and comes short again and again, because there is no effort without error and shortcoming; but who does actually strive to do the deeds; who knows the great enthusiasms, the great devotions; who spends himself in a worthy cause; who at the best knows in the end the triumph of high achievement, and who at the worst, if he fails, at least fails while daring greatly, so that his place shall never be with those cold and timid souls who know neither victory nor defeat. Shame on the man of cultivated taste who permits refinement to develop into a fastidiousness that unfits him for doing the rough work of a workaday world. Among the free peoples who govern themselves there is but a small field of usefulness open for the men of cloistered life who shrink from contact with their fellows. Still less room is there for those who deride or slight what is done by those who actually bear the brunt of the day; nor yet for those others who always profess that they would like to take action, if only the conditions of life were not what they actually are. The man who does nothing cuts the same sordid figure in the pages of history, whether he be cynic, or fop, or voluptuary. There is little use for the being whose tepid soul knows nothing of the great and generous emotion, of the high pride, the stern belief, the lofty enthusiasm, of the men who quell the storm and ride the thunder. Well for these men if they succeed; well also, though not so well, if they fail, given only that they have nobly ventured, and have put forth all their heart and strength. It is warworn Hotspur, spent with hard fighting, he of the many errors and the valiant end, over whose memory we love to linger, not over the memory of the young lord who "but for the vile guns would have been a soldier."

Theodore Roosevelt

Invictus

Out of the night that covers me,
> Black as the Pit from pole to pole,
I thank whatever gods may be
> For my unconquerable soul.

In the fell clutch of circumstance
> I have not winced nor cried aloud.
Under the bludgeonings of chance
> My head is bloody, but unbowed.

Beyond this place of wrath and tears
> Looms but the Horror of the shade,
And yet the menace of the years
> Finds, and shall find, me unafraid.

It matters not how strait the gate,
> How charged with punishments the scroll,
I am the master of my fate:
> I am the captain of my soul.

William Ernest Henley

STRIVE

from Of Experience

He who fears he shall suffer, already suffers what he fears.

Michel de Montaigne

from As a Man Thinketh

Calmness of mind is one of the beautiful jewels of wisdom. It is the result of long and patient effort in self-control. Its presence is an indication of ripened experience, and of a more than ordinary knowledge of the laws and operations of thought.

A man becomes calm in the measure that he understands himself as a thought-evolved being, for such knowledge necessitates the understanding of others as the result of thought, and as he develops a right understanding, and sees more and more clearly the internal relations of things by the action of cause and effect, he ceases to fuss and fume and worry and grieve, and remains poised, steadfast, serene.

The calm man, having learned how to govern himself, knows how to adapt himself to others; and they, in turn, reverence his spiritual strength, and feel that they can learn of him and rely upon him. The more tranquil a man becomes, the greater is his success, his influence, his power for good. Even the ordinary trader will find his business prosperity increase as he develops a greater self-control and equanimity, for people will always prefer to deal with a man whose demeanour is strongly equable.

The strong, calm man is always loved and revered. He is like a shade-giving tree in a thirsty land, or a sheltering rock in a storm. "Who does not love a tranquil heart, a sweet-tempered, balanced life? It does not matter whether it rains or shines, or what changes come to those possessing these blessings, for they are always sweet, serene, and calm. That exquisite poise of character which we call serenity is the last lesson of culture; it is the flowering of life, the fruitage of the soul. It is precious as wisdom, more to be desired than gold—yea, than even fine gold. How insignificant mere money-seeking looks in comparison with a serene life—a life that dwells in the ocean of Truth, beneath the waves, beyond the reach of tempests, in the Eternal Calm!

"How many people we know who sour their lives, who ruin all that is sweet and beautiful by explosive tempers, who destroy their poise of character, and make bad blood! It is a question whether the great majority of people do not ruin their lives and mar their happiness by lack of self-control. How few people we meet in life who are well-balanced, who have that exquisite poise which is characteristic of the finished character!"

Yes, humanity surges with uncontrolled passion, is tumultuous with ungoverned grief, is blown about by anxiety and doubt. Only the wise man, only he whose thoughts are controlled and purified, makes the winds and the storms of the soul obey him.

Tempest-tossed souls, wherever ye may be, under whatsoever conditions ye may live, know this—in the ocean of life the isles of Blessedness are smiling, and the sunny shore of your ideal awaits your coming. Keep your hand firmly upon the helm of thought. In the barque of your soul reclines the commanding Master; He does but sleep; wake Him. Self-control is strength; Right Thought is mastery; Calmness is power. Say unto your heart, "Peace, be still!"

James Allen

from The Prophet

Then a woman said, Speak to us of Joy and Sorrow.

And he answered:

Your joy is your sorrow unmasked.

And the selfsame well from which your laughter rises was oftentimes filled with your tears.

And how else can it be?

The deeper that sorrow carves into your being, the more joy you can contain.

Is not the cup that holds your wine the very cup that was burned in the potter's oven?

And is not the lute that soothes your spirit, the very wood that was hollowed with knives?

When you are joyous, look deep into your heart and you shall find it is only that which has given you sorrow that is giving you joy.

When you are sorrowful look again in your heart, and you shall see that in truth you are weeping for that which has been your delight.

Some of you say, "Joy is greater than sorrow," and others say, "Nay, sorrow is the greater."

But I say unto you, they are inseparable.

Together they come, and when one sits alone with you at your board, remember that the other is asleep upon your bed.

Verily you are suspended like scales between your sorrow and your joy.
Only when you are empty are you at standstill and balanced.
When the treasure-keeper lifts you to weigh his gold and his silver, needs must your joy or your sorrow rise or fall.

Kahlil Gibran

from Adam Bede

Men's muscles move better when their souls are making merry music.

George Eliot

from War and Peace

The strongest of all warriors are these two—time and patience.

Leo Tolstoy

from The Encheiridion

Some things are under our control, while others are not under our control. Under our control are conception, choice, desire, aversion, and, in a word, everything that is our own doing; not under our control are our body, our property, reputation, office, and, in a word, everything that is not our own doing. Furthermore, the things under our control are by nature free, unhindered, and unimpeded; while the things not under our control are weak, servile, subject to hindrance, and not our own. Remember, therefore, that if what is naturally slavish you think to be free, and what is not your own to be your own, you will be hampered, will grieve, will be in turmoil, and will blame both gods and men; while if you think only what is your own to be your own, and what is not your own to be, as it really is, not your own, then no one will ever be able to exert compulsion upon you, no one will hinder you, you will blame no one, will find fault with no one, will do absolutely nothing against your will, you will have no personal enemy, no one will harm you, for neither is there any harm that can touch you.

With such high aims, therefore, remember that you must bestir yourself with no slight effort to lay hold of them, but you will have to give up some things entirely, and defer others for the time being. But if you wish for these things also, and at the same time for both office and wealth, it may be that you will not get even these latter, because you aim also at the former, and certainly you will fail to get the former, which alone bring freedom and happiness.

Make it, therefore, your study at the very outset to say to every harsh external impression, "You are an external impression and not at all what you appear to be." After that, examine it and test it by these rules which you have, the first and most important of which is this: Whether the impression has to do with the things which are under our control, or with those which are not under our control; and, if it has to do with some one of the things not under our control, have ready to hand the answer, "It is nothing to me."

Epictetus

from Walden

Let us spend one day as deliberately as nature, and not be thrown off the track by every nutshell and mosquito's wing that falls on the rails. Let us rise early and fast, or break fast, gently and without perturbation; let company come and let company go, let the bells ring and the children cry – determined to make a day of it. Why should we knock under and go with the stream? Let us not be upset and overwhelmed in that terrible rapid and whirlpool called a dinner, situated in the meridian shallows. Weather this danger and you are safe, for the rest of the way is downhill. With unrelaxed nerves, with morning vigour, sail by it, looking another way, tied to the mast like Ulysses. If the engine whistles, let it whistle till it is hoarse for its pains. If the bell rings, why should we run? We will consider what kind of music they are like. Let us settle ourselves, and work and wedge our feet downward through the mud and slush of opinion, and prejudice, and tradition, and delusion, and appearance, that alluvion which covers the globe, through Paris and London, through New York and Boston and

Concord, through church and state, through poetry and philosophy and religion, till we come to a hard bottom and rocks in place, which we can call *reality*, and say, This is, and no mistake; and then begin, having a *point d'appui*, below freshet and frost and fire, a place where you might found a wall or a state, or set a lamp-post safely, or perhaps a gauge, not a Nilometer, but a Realometer, that future ages might know how deep a freshet of shams and appearances had gathered from time to time. If you stand right fronting and face to face to a fact, you will see the sun glimmer on both its surfaces, as if it were a scimitar, and feel its sweet edge dividing you through the heart and marrow, and so you will happily conclude your mortal career. Be it life or death, we crave only reality. If we are really dying, let us hear the rattle in our throats and feel cold in the extremities; if we are alive, let us go about our business.

Time is but the stream I go a-fishing in. I drink at it; but while I drink I see the sandy bottom and detect how shallow it is. Its thin current slides away, but eternity remains. I would drink deeper; fish in the sky, whose bottom is pebbly with stars. I cannot count one. I know not the first letter of the alphabet. I have always been regretting that I was not as wise as the day I was born. The intellect is a cleaver; it discerns and rifts its way into the secret of things. I do not wish to be any more busy with my hands than is necessary. My head is hands and feet. I feel all my best faculties concentrated in it. My instinct tells me that my head is an organ for burrowing, as some creatures use their snout and forepaws, and with it I would mine and burrow my way through these hills. I think that the richest vein is somewhere hereabouts; so by the divining-rod and thin rising vapours I judge; and here I will begin to mine.

Henry David Thoreau

from What I Think and Feel at 25

I am twenty-five years old. I wish I had ten million dollars, and never had to do another lick of work as long as I live.

But as I *do* have to keep at it, I might as well declare that the chief thing I've learned so far is: If you don't know much—well, nobody else knows much more. And nobody knows half as much about your own interests as *you* know.

If you believe in anything very strongly—including yourself—and if you go after that thing alone, you end up in jail, in heaven, in the headlines, or in the largest house in the block, according to what you started after. If you *don't* believe in anything very strongly—including yourself—you go along, and enough money is made out of you to buy an automobile for some other fellow's son, and you marry if you've got time, and if you do you have a lot of children, whether you have time or not, and finally you get tired and you die.

If you're in the second of those two classes

you have the most fun before you're twenty-five. If you're in the first, you have it afterward.

You see, if you're in the first class you'll frequently be called a darn fool—or worse. That was as true in Philadelphia about 1727 as it is to-day. Anybody knows that a kid that walked around town munching a loaf of bread and not caring what anybody thought was a darn fool. It stands to reason! But there are a lot of darn fools who get their pictures in the schoolbooks—with their names under the pictures. And the sensible fellows, the ones that had time to laugh, well, their pictures are in there, too. But their *names* aren't—and the laughs look sort of frozen on their faces.

The particular sort of darn fool I mean ought to remember that he's *least* a darn fool when he's being *called* a darn fool. The main thing is to be your own kind of a darn fool.

(The above advice is of course only for darn fools *under* twenty-five. It may be all wrong for darn fools over twenty-five.)

F. Scott Fitzgerald

from The Life of Petrarch by S. Dobson

These friends of mine regard the pleasures of the world as the supreme good; they do not comprehend that it is possible to renounce these pleasures. They are ignorant of my resources. I have friends whose society is delightful to me; they are persons of all countries and of all ages; distinguished in war, in council, and in letters; easy to live with, always at my command. They come at my call, and return when I desire them: they are never out of humour, and they answer all my questions with readiness. Some present in review before me the events of past ages; others reveal to me the secrets of Nature: these teach me how to live, and those how to die: these dispel my melancholy by their mirth, and amuse me by their sallies of wit: and some there are who prepare my soul to suffer everything, to desire nothing, and to become thoroughly acquainted with itself. In a word, they open a door to all the arts and sciences. As a reward for such great services, they require only a corner of my little house, where they may be safely sheltered from the depredations of their enemies. In fine, I carry them with me into the fields, the silence of which suits them better than the business and tumults of cities.

Petrarch

As You Go Through Life

Don't look for the flaws as you go through life;
    And even when you find them,
It is wise and kind to be somewhat blind,
    And look for the virtue behind them;
For the cloudiest night has a hint of light
    Somewhere in its shadows hiding:
It's better by far to hunt for a star,
    Than the spots on the sun abiding.

The current of life runs ever away
    To the bosom of God's great ocean.
Don't set your force 'gainst the river's course,
    And think to alter its motion.
Don't waste a curse on the universe,
    Remember, it lived before you:
Don't butt at the storm with your puny form,
    But bend and let it go o'er you.

The world will never adjust itself
    To suit your whims to the letter,
Some things must go wrong, your whole life long,
    And the sooner you know it the better.

It is folly to fight with the Infinite,
>   And go under at last in the wrestle.
The wiser man shapes into God's plan,
>   As water shapes into a vessel.

Ella Wheeler Wilcox

from Meditations

Begin the morning by saying to thyself, I shall meet with the busybody, the ungrateful, arrogant, deceitful, envious, unsocial. All these things happen to them by reason of their ignorance of what is good and evil. But I who have seen the nature of the good that it is beautiful, and of the bad that it is ugly, and the nature of him who does wrong, that it is akin to me, not [only] of the same blood or seed, but that it participates in [the same] intelligence and [the same] portion of the divinity, I can neither be injured by any of them, for no one can fix on me what is ugly, nor can I be angry with my kinsman, nor hate him. For we are made for co-operation, like feet, like hands, like eyelids, like the rows of the upper and lower teeth. To act against one another then is contrary to nature; and it is acting against one another to be vexed and to turn away.

Marcus Aurelius

from Ginger Snaps

Did you never *wish* you had it? Of course you have, a thousand times. You never would be miserable any more if it could only be so. You are sure of that. It may be a fine house, a fine store, a fine carriage. No matter what; the desire for it has taken the spice and flavor out of every blessing you possess. I used to play with a little girl once, who told me in confidence, and in pantalettes, "that she should never be happy till she had a real *true* gold watch; and that she meant to be married, as soon as ever she could, to a rich man who would give her one." For myself, I had much rather at that time have had a bunch of flowers, and I didn't suppose she really meant what she said, as she stood there tying on her doll's bonnet. But she was in dead earnest, though I *didn't* know it. Sure enough, she got her rich husband, and her gold watch; and was sick enough of both, as I have since found out, before the honeymoon was well over.

One day I heard a boy say to his younger brother, who was crying lustily, "Now, Tom, I know you don't want anything, but what do you *think* you want?" That boy was a philosopher, and went to the root of the matter. It is not what we really want, but what we *think* we want, that frets most of us. Perhaps you tell me that you suffer just as much as if your longing were a reasonable or a sensible one. That's true too; but if you only could snatch *to-day's* legitimate happiness, instead of wondering if you could not get a great deal more, for that to-morrow which may never come to you, wouldn't it be wiser? The other day I went off into the woods, with a dear little girl, who is much more of a poetess than a philosopher. Not a patch of soft green moss, not the tiniest bud of a wild flower, or flitting butterfly, or bird, or tree-shadow on the smooth clear lake, escaped her bright, glad eyes. The *first* flower she found enraptured her, and she climbed quite a steep rock with her mites of feet for the second, and so on till her tiny hands were full. Just then she found quite a bunch of bright pink blossoms; and I was so glad for her; when suddenly she burst into such a grieved, piteous cry, "Oh dear! oh dear! what *shall* I do? *I can't hold them all.*"

If we'd only think of that! That "we can't hold

them all." That in order to grasp that which is the moment's wish, we must let something else drop that we prize. Something that we can never retrace our steps, in life's devious paths, to reclaim. It may be health, or character, or life itself, for that which is so perishable, so unsatisfying, so harmful, that we can never cease wondering how the "glamour" of it could have so dazzled our mental and moral vision. The little child I speak of, who clambered up the rock to secure that *one* flower, was happier in its possession than with the myriads that she afterwards found lying at her very feet. She had *earned* that one! She had encountered a fierce briarbush; she had got her hands scratched in the conflict; she had tickled her little nose with a defiant twig; she had tangled her curls; she had scraped her little fat knee till it was red — and *got it!* All herself, too! I couldn't elaborate a better moral, if I preached an hour. We don't value happiness in heaps. It is the one little sweet blossom, that comes unexpectedly in our way, that we love best after all. Isn't it so?

Fanny Fern

Courage

If in the past should brooding sorrow dwell
    Look not that way,
Let not the echoes of a tolling bell
    Ring in another day.
Be brave in thought—the fearless thought shall lead
To the achievement of the fearless deed.

Ella Fuller Maitland

from Leaves of Grass

This is what you shall do: Love the earth and sun and the animals, despise riches, give alms to every one that asks, stand up for the stupid and crazy, devote your income and labor to others, hate tyrants, argue not concerning God, have patience and indulgence toward the people, take off your hat to nothing known or unknown or to any man or number of men, go freely with powerful uneducated persons and with the young and with the mothers of families, read these leaves in the open air every season of every year of your life, reexamine all you have been told at school or church or in any book, dismiss whatever insults your own soul, and your very flesh shall be a great poem and have the richest fluency not only in its words but in the silent lines of its lips and face and between the lashes of your eyes and in every motion and joint of your body.

Walt Whitman

The Golden Windows

All day long the little boy worked hard, in field and barn and shed, for his people were poor farmers, and could not pay a workman; but at sunset there came an hour that was all his own, for his father had given it to him. Then the boy would go up to the top of a hill and look across at another hill that rose some miles away. On this far hill stood a house with windows of clear gold and diamonds. They shone and blazed so that it made the boy wink to look at them: but after a while the people in the house put up shutters, as it seemed, and then it looked like any common farmhouse. The boy supposed they did this because it was supper-time; and then he would go into the house and have his supper of bread and milk, and so to bed.

One day the boy's father called him and said: "You have been a good boy, and have earned a holiday. Take this day for your own; but remember that God gave it, and try to learn some good thing."

The boy thanked his father and kissed his mother; then he put a piece of bread in his pocket, and started off to find the house with the golden windows.

It was pleasant walking. His bare feet made marks in the white dust, and when he looked back, the footprints seemed to be following him, and making company for him. His shadow, too, kept beside him, and would dance or run with him as he pleased; so it was very cheerful.

By and by he felt hungry; and he sat down by a brown brook that ran through the alder hedge by the roadside, and ate his bread, and drank the clear water. Then he scattered the crumbs for the birds, as his mother had taught him to do, and went on his way.

After a long time he came to a high green hill; and when he had climbed the hill, there was the house on the top; but it seemed that the shutters were up, for he could not see the golden windows. He came up to the house, and then he could well have wept, for the windows were of clear glass, like any others, and there was no gold anywhere about them.

A woman came to the door, and looked kindly at the boy, and asked him what he wanted.

"I saw the golden windows from our hilltop,"

he said, "and I came to see them, but now they are only glass."

The woman shook her head and laughed.

"We are poor farming people," she said, "and are not likely to have gold about our windows; but glass is better to see through."

She bade the boy sit down on the broad stone step at the door, and brought him a cup of milk and a cake, and bade him rest; then she called her daughter, a child of his own age, and nodded kindly at the two, and went back to her work.

The little girl was barefooted like himself, and wore a brown cotton gown, but her hair was golden like the windows he had seen, and her eyes were blue like the sky at noon. She led the boy about the farm, and showed him her black calf with the white star on its forehead, and he told her about his own at home, which was red like a chestnut, with four white feet. Then when they had eaten an apple together, and so had become friends, the boy asked her about the golden windows. The little girl nodded, and said she knew all about them, only he had mistaken the house.

"You have come quite the wrong way!" she

said. "Come with me, and I will show you the house with the golden windows, and then you will see for yourself."

They went to a knoll that rose behind the farmhouse, and as they went the little girl told him that the golden windows could only be seen at a certain hour, about sunset.

"Yes, I know that!" said the boy.

When they reached the top of the knoll, the girl turned and pointed; and there on a hill far away stood a house with windows of clear gold and diamond, just as he had seen them. And when they looked again, the boy saw that it was his own home.

Then he told the little girl that he must go; and he gave her his best pebble, the white one with the red band, that he had carried for a year in his pocket; and she gave him three horse-chestnuts, one red like satin, one spotted, and one white like milk. He kissed her, and promised to come again, but he did not tell her what he had learned; and so he went back down the hill, and the little girl stood in the sunset light and watched him.

The way home was long, and it was dark

before the boy reached his father's house; but the lamplight and firelight shone through the windows, making them almost as bright as he had seen them from the hilltop; and when he opened the door, his mother came to kiss him, and his little sister ran to throw her arms about his neck, and his father looked up and smiled from his seat by the fire.

"Have you had a good day?" asked his mother.

Yes, the boy had had a very good day.

"And have you learned anything?" asked his father.

"Yes!" said the boy. "I have learned that our house has windows of gold and diamond."

Laura E. Richards

FIND

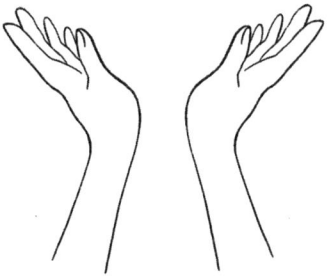

from Eleanora

They who dream by day are cognizant of many things which escape those who dream only by night.

Edgar Allan Poe

Barter

Life has loveliness to sell,
    All beautiful and splendid things,
Blue waves whitened on a cliff,
    Soaring fire that sways and sings,
And children's faces looking up
Holding wonder like a cup.

Life has loveliness to sell,
    Music like a curve of gold,
Scent of pine trees in the rain,
    Eyes that love you, arms that hold,
And for your spirit's still delight,
Holy thoughts that star the night.

Spend all you have for loveliness,
    Buy it and never count the cost;
For one white singing hour of peace
    Count many a year of strife well lost,
And for a breath of ecstasy
Give all you have been, or could be.

Sara Teasdale

from Marriage and Love

Man has bought brains, but all the millions in the world have failed to buy love. Man has subdued bodies, but all the power on earth has been unable to subdue love. Man has conquered whole nations, but all his armies could not conquer love. Man has chained and fettered the spirit, but he has been utterly helpless before love. High on a throne, with all the splendor and pomp his gold can command, man is yet poor and desolate, if love passes him by. And if it stays, the poorest hovel is radiant with warmth, with life and color. Thus love has the magic power to make of a beggar a king. Yes, love is free; it can dwell in no other atmosphere. In freedom it gives itself unreservedly, abundantly, completely. All the laws on the statutes, all the courts in the universe, cannot tear it from the soil, once love has taken root.

Emma Goldman

from What Is to Be Done?

The vocation of every man and woman is to serve other people.

Leo Tolstoy

If I can stop one heart from breaking

If I can stop one heart from breaking,
I shall not live in vain;
If I can ease one life the aching,
Or cool one pain,
Or help one fainting robin
Unto his nest again,
I shall not live in vain.

Emily Dickinson

Letter to Sara Hennell

You will soon be settled and enjoying the blessed spring and summer time. I hope you are looking forward to it with as much delight as I. One has to spend so many years in learning how to be happy. I am just beginning to make some progress in the science, and I hope to disprove Young's theory that "as soon as we have found the key of life, it opes the gates of death." Every year strips us of at least one vain expectation, and teaches us to reckon some solid good in its stead. I never will believe that our youngest days are our happiest. What a miserable augury for the progress of the race and the destination of the individual, if the more matured and enlightened state is the less happy one! Childhood is only the beautiful and happy time in contemplation and retrospect: to the child it is full of deep sorrows, the meaning of which is unknown. Witness colic and whooping-cough and dread of ghosts, to say nothing of hell and Satan, and an offended Deity in the sky, who was angry when I wanted too much plum-cake. Then the sorrows of older persons, which children see but cannot understand, are worse than all. All this to prove that we are happier than when we were seven years old, and that we shall be happier when we are forty than we are now, which I call a comfortable doctrine, and one worth trying to believe! I am sitting with father, who every now and then jerks off my attention to the history of Queen Elizabeth, which he is reading.

George Eliot

Letter to Menoeceus

So every pleasure is a good thing because its nature is favorable to us, yet not every pleasure is to be chosen — just as every pain is a bad thing, yet not every pain is always to be shunned. It is proper to make all these decisions through measuring things side by side and looking at both the advantages and disadvantages, for sometimes we treat a good thing as bad and a bad thing as good.

Fourth, we hold that self-reliance is a great good — not so that we will always have only a few things but so that if we do not have much we will rejoice in the few things we have, firmly persuaded that those who need luxury the least enjoy it the most, and that everything natural is easily obtained whereas everything groundless is hard to get. So simple flavors bring just as much pleasure as a fancy diet if all pain from true need has been removed, and bread and water give the highest pleasure when someone in need partakes of them. Training yourself to live simply and without luxury brings you complete health, gives you endless energy to face the necessities of life, better prepares you for the occasional luxury, and makes you fearless no matter your fortune in life.

So when we say that pleasure is the goal, we do not mean the pleasure of decadent people and lying in a bed of desire, as is believed by those who are ignorant or who don't understand us or who are ill-disposed to us, but to be free from bodily pain and mental disturbance. For a pleasant life is produced not by drinking and endless parties and bedding boys and women and consuming fish and other delicacies of an extravagant table, but by sober reasoning, searching out the cause of everything we accept or reject, and driving out opinions that cause the greatest trouble in the soul.

Epicurus

from Emma

"There is no charm equal to tenderness of heart,"

Jane Austen

from Friendship

We have a great deal more kindness than is ever spoken. Maugre all the selfishness that chills like east winds the world, the whole human family is bathed with an element of love like a fine ether. How many persons we meet in houses, whom we scarcely speak to, whom yet we honor, and who honor us! How many we see in the street, or sit with in church, whom, though silently, we warmly rejoice to be with! Read the language of these wandering eye-beams. The heart knoweth.

The effect of the indulgence of this human affection is a certain cordial exhilaration. In poetry and in common speech, the emotions of benevolence and complacency which are felt towards others are likened to the material effects of fire; so swift, or much more swift, more active, more cheering, are these fine inward irradiations. From the highest degree of passionate love, to the lowest degree of good will, they make the sweetness of life.

Our intellectual and active powers increase with our affection. The scholar sits down to write, and all his years of meditation do not furnish him with one good thought or happy expression; but it is necessary to write a letter to a friend,—and forthwith troops of gentle thoughts invest themselves, on every hand, with chosen words. See, in any house where virtue and self-respect abide, the palpitation which the approach of a stranger causes. A commended stranger is expected and announced, and an uneasiness betwixt pleasure and pain invades all the hearts of a household. His arrival almost brings fear to the good hearts that would welcome him. The house is dusted, all things fly into their places, the old coat is exchanged for the new, and they must get up a dinner if they can. Of a commended stranger, only the good report is told by others, only the good and new is heard by us. He stands to us for humanity. He is what we wish. Having imagined and invested him, we ask how we should stand related in conversation and action with such a man, and are uneasy with fear. The same idea exalts conversation with him. We talk better than we are wont. We have the nimblest fancy, a richer memory, and our dumb devil has taken leave for the time. For long hours we can continue a series of sincere, graceful, rich communications, drawn from the oldest, secretest experience so that they who sit by, of our own kinsfolk and acquaintance, shall feel a lively surprise at our unusual powers. But as soon as the stranger begins to intrude his partialities, his definitions, his defects, into the conversation, it is all over. He has heard the first, the last and best, he will ever hear from us. He is no stranger now. Vulgarity, ignorance, misapprehension, are old acquaintances. Now, when he comes, he may get the order, the dress, and the dinner,—but the throbbing of the heart, and the communications of the soul, no more.

Pleasant are these jets of affection, which relume a young world for me again. Delicious is a just and firm encounter of two in a thought, in a feeling. How beautiful, on their approach to this beating heart, the steps and forms of the gifted and the true! The moment we indulge our affections, the earth is metamorphosed: there is no winter, and no night: all tragedies, all ennuis vanish; all duties even; nothing fills the proceeding eternity but the forms all radiant of beloved persons. Let the soul be assured that somewhere in the universe it should rejoin its friend, and it would be content and cheerful alone for a thousand years.

Ralph Waldo Emerson

from On the Happy Life

What is the happy life? It is peace of mind, and lasting tranquillity. This will be yours if you possess greatness of soul; it will be yours if you possess the steadfastness that resolutely clings to a good judgment just reached. How does a man reach this condition? By gaining a complete view of truth, by maintaining, in all that he does, order, measure, fitness, and a will that is inoffensive and kindly, that is intent upon reason and never departs therefrom, that commands at the same time love and admiration. In short, to give you the principle in brief compass, the wise man's soul ought to be such as would be proper for a god. What more can one desire who possesses all honourable things? For if dishonourable things can contribute to the best estate, then there will be the possibility of a happy life under conditions which do not include an honourable life. And what is more base or foolish than to connect the good of a rational soul with things irrational? Yet there are certain philosophers who hold that the Supreme Good admits of increase because it is hardly complete when the gifts of fortune are adverse. Even Antipater, one of the great leaders of this school, admits that he ascribes some influence to externals, though only a very slight influence. You see, however, what absurdity lies in not being content with the daylight unless it is increased by a tiny fire. What importance can a spark have in the midst of this clear sunlight?

Lucius Annaeus Seneca

I wandered lonely as a Cloud

I wandered lonely as a Cloud
That floats on high o'er vales and hills,
When all at once I saw a crowd,
A host of golden Daffodils;
Beside the Lake, beneath the trees,
Fluttering and dancing in the breeze.

Continuous as the stars that shine
And twinkle on the milky way,
They stretched in never-ending line
Along the margin of a bay:
Ten thousand saw I at a glance,
Tossing their heads in sprightly dance.

The waves beside them danced, but they
Out-did the sparkling waves in glee:—
A poet could not but be gay,
In such a jocund company;
I gazed—and gazed—but little thought
What wealth the show to me had brought:

For oft, when on my couch I lie
In vacant or in pensive mood,
They flash upon that inward eye
Which is the bliss of solitude,
And then my heart with pleasure fills,
And dances with the Daffodils.

William Wordsworth

Letter to W. S. Williams

In the matter of friendship, I have observed that disappointment arises chiefly, not from liking our friends too well, or thinking of them too highly, but rather from an over-estimate of *their* liking for and opinion of *us*, and that if we guard ourselves with sufficient scrupulousness of care from error in this direction, and can be content, and even happy to give more affection than we receive—can make just comparison of circumstances, and be severely accurate in drawing inferences, and never let self-love blind our eyes—then I think we may manage to get through life with consistency and constancy, unembittered by that misanthropy which springs from revulsion of feeling. The moral is, that if we would build on a sure foundation in friendship, we must love our friends for *their* sakes rather than for *our* own.

Charlotte Brontë

from Fashions in Literature

The pursuit of happiness! It is not strange that men call it an illusion. But I am well satisfied that it is not the thing itself, but the pursuit, that is an illusion. Instead of thinking of the pursuit, why not fix our thoughts upon the moments, the hours, perhaps the days, of this divine peace, this merriment of body and mind, that can be repeated and perhaps indefinitely extended by the simplest of all means, namely, a disposition to make the best of whatever comes to us? Perhaps the Latin poet was right in saying that no man can count himself happy while in this life, that is, in a continuous state of happiness; but as there is for the soul no time save the conscious moment called "now," it is quite possible to make that "now" a happy state of existence. The point I make is that we should not habitually postpone that season of happiness to the future.

Charles Dudley Warner

A Psalm of Life

Tell me not, in mournful numbers,
    "Life is but an empty dream!"
For the soul is dead that slumbers,
    And things are not what they seem.

Life is real! Life is earnest!
    And the grave is not its goal;
"Dust thou art, to dust returnest,"
    Was not spoken of the soul.

Not enjoyment, and not sorrow,
    Is our destined end or way;
But to act, that each to-morrow
    Find us farther than to-day.

Art is long, and Time is fleeting,
    And our hearts, though stout and brave,
Still, like muffled drums, are beating
    Funeral marches to the grave.

    In the world's broad field of battle,
        In the bivouac of Life,

Be not like dumb, driven cattle;
>   Be a hero in the strife!

Trust no Future, howe'er pleasant!
>   Let the dead Past bury its dead!
Act, — act in the living Present!
>   Heart within, and God o'erhead!

Lives of great men all remind us
>   We can make our lives sublime,
And, departing, leave behind us
>   Footprints on the sands of time;

Footprints, that perhaps another,
>   Sailing o'er life's solemn main,
A forlorn and shipwrecked brother,
>   Seeing, shall take heart again.

Let us, then, be up and doing,
>   With a heart for any fate;
Still achieving, still pursuing,
>   Learn to labor and to wait.

Henry Wadsworth Longfellow

Who Owns the Mountains?

It was the little lad that asked the question; and the answer also, as you will see, was mainly his.

We had been keeping Sunday afternoon together in our favourite fashion, following out that pleasant text which tells us to "behold the fowls of the air." There is no injunction of Holy Writ less burdensome in acceptance, or more profitable in obedience, than this easy out-of-doors commandment. For several hours we walked in the way of this precept, through the untangled woods that lie behind the Forest Hills Lodge, where a pair of pigeon-hawks had their nest; and around the brambly shores of the small pond, where Maryland yellow-throats and song-sparrows were settled; and under the lofty hemlocks of the fragment of forest across the road, where rare warblers flitted silently among the tree-tops. The light beneath the evergreens was growing dim as we came out from their shadow into the widespread glow of the sunset, on the edge of a grassy hill, overlooking the long valley of the Gale River, and uplooking to the Franconia Mountains.

It was the benediction hour. The placid air of the day shed a new tranquility over the consoling landscape. The heart of the earth seemed to taste a repose more perfect than that of common days. A hermit-thrush, far up the vale, sang his vesper hymn; while the swallows, seeking their evening meal, circled above the riverfields without an effort, twittering softly, now and then, as if they must give thanks. Slight and indefinable touches in the scene, perhaps the mere absence of the tiny human figures passing along the road or laboring in the distant meadows, perhaps the blue curls of smoke rising lazily from the farmhouse chimneys, or the family groups sitting under the maple-trees before the door, diffused a Sabbath atmosphere over the world.

Then said the lad, lying on the grass beside me, "Father, who owns the mountains?"

I happened to have heard, the day before, of two or three lumber companies that had bought some of the woodland slopes; so I told him their names, adding that there were probably a good many different owners, whose claims taken all together would cover the whole Franconia range of hills.

"Well," answered the lad, after a moment of silence, "I don't see what difference that makes. Everybody can look at them."

They lay stretched out before us in the level sunlight, the sharp peaks outlined against the sky, the vast ridges of forest sinking smoothly towards the valleys, the deep hollows gathering purple shadows in their bosoms, and the little foothills standing out in rounded promontories of brighter green from the darker mass behind them.

Far to the east, the long comb of Twin Mountain extended itself back into the untrodden wilderness. Mount Garfield lifted a clear-cut pyramid through the translucent air. The huge bulk of Lafayette ascended majestically in front of us, crowned with a rosy diadem of rocks. Eagle Cliff and Bald Mountain stretched their line of scalloped peaks across the entrance to the Notch. Beyond that shadowy vale, the swelling summits of Cannon Mountain rolled away to meet the tumbling waves of Kinsman, dominated by one loftier crested billow that seemed almost ready to curl and break out of green silence into snowy foam. Far down the sleeping Landaff valley the undulating dome of Moosilauke trembled in the distant blue.

They were all ours, from crested cliff to wooded base. The solemn groves of firs and spruces, the plumed sierras of lofty pines, the stately pillared forests of birch and beech, the wild ravines, the tremulous thickets of silvery poplar, the bare peaks with their wide outlooks, and the cool vales resounding with the ceaseless song of little rivers,—we knew and loved them all; they ministered peace and joy to us; they were all ours, though we held no title-deeds and our ownership had never been recorded.

What is property, after all? The law says there are two kinds, real and personal. But it seems to me that the only real property is that which is truly personal, that which we take into our inner life and make our own forever, by understanding and admiration and sympathy and love. This is the only kind of possession that is worth anything.

A gallery of great paintings adorns the house of the Honourable Midas Bond, and every year adds a new treasure to his collection. He knows how much they cost him, and he keeps the run of the quotations at the auction sales, congratulating himself as the price of the works of his well-chosen artists rises in the scale, and the value of his art treasures is enhanced. But why should he call them his? He is only their custodian. He keeps them well varnished, and framed in gilt. But he never passes through those gilded frames into the world of beauty that lies behind the painted canvas. He knows nothing of those lovely places from which the artist's soul and hand have drawn their inspiration. They are closed and barred to him. He has bought the pictures, but he cannot buy the key. The poor art student who wanders through his gallery, lingering with awe and love before the masterpieces, owns them far more truly than Midas does.

Pomposus Silverman purchased a rich library a few years ago. The books were rare and costly. That was the reason why Pomposus bought them. He was proud to feel that he was the possessor of literary treasures which were not to be found in the houses of his wealthiest acquaintances. But the threadbare Bücherfreund, who was engaged at a slender salary to catalogue the library and take care of it, became the real proprietor. Pomposus paid for the books, but Bücherfreund enjoyed them.

I do not mean to say that the possession of much money is always a barrier to real wealth of mind and heart. Nor would I maintain that all the poor of this world are rich in faith and heirs of the kingdom. But some of them are. And if some of the rich of this world (through the grace of Him with whom all things are possible) are also modest in their tastes, and gentle in their hearts, and open in their minds, and ready to be pleased with unbought pleasures, they simply share in the best things which are provided for all.

I speak not now of the strife that men wage over the definition and the laws of property. Doubtless there is much here that needs to be set right. There are men and women in the world who are shut out from the right to earn a living, so poor that they must perish for want of daily bread, so full of misery that there is no room for the tiniest seed of joy in their lives. This is the lingering shame of civilisation. Some day, perhaps, we shall find the way to banish it. Some day, every man shall have his title to a share in the world's great work and the world's large joy.

But meantime it is certain that, where there are a hundred poor bodies who suffer from physical privation, there are a thousand poor souls who suffer from spiritual poverty. To relieve this greater suffering there needs no change of laws, only a change of heart.

What does it profit a man to be the landed proprietor of countless acres unless he can reap the harvest of delight that blooms from every rood of God's earth for the seeing eye and the loving spirit? And who can reap that harvest so closely that there shall not be abundant gleaning left for all mankind? The most that a wide estate can yield to its legal owner is a living. But the real owner can gather from a field of goldenrod, shining in the August sunlight, an unearned increment of delight.

We measure success by accumulation. The measure is false. The true measure is appreciation. He who loves most has most.

How foolishly we train ourselves for the work of life! We give our most arduous and eager efforts to the cultivation of those faculties which will serve us in the competitions of the forum and the market-place. But if we were wise, we should care infinitely more for the unfolding of those inward, secret, spiritual powers by which alone we can become the owners of anything that is worth having. Surely God is the great proprietor. Yet all His works He has given away. He holds no title-deeds. The one thing that is His, is the perfect understanding, the perfect joy, the perfect love, of all things that He has made. To a share in this high ownership He welcomes all who are poor in spirit. This is the earth which the meek inherit. This is the patrimony of the saints in light.

"Come, laddie," I said to my comrade, "let us go home. You and I are very rich. We own the mountains. But we can never sell them, and we don't want to."

Henry Van Dyke

FLOURISH

Your World

Your world is as big as you make it.
I know, for I used to abide
In the narrowest nest in a corner,
My wings pressing close to my side.

But I sighted the distant horizon
Where the skyline encircled the sea
And I throbbed with a burning desire
To travel this immensity.

I battered the cordons around me
And cradled my wings on the breeze,
Then soared to the uttermost reaches
With rapture, with power, with ease!

Georgia Douglas Johnson

Advice to Youth

Being told I would be expected to talk here, I inquired what sort of a talk I ought to make. They said it should be something suitable to youth—something didactic, instructive, or something in the nature of good advice. Very well. I have a few things in my mind which I have often longed to say for the instruction of the young; for it is in one's tender early years that such things will best take root and be most enduring and most valuable. First, then, I will say to you, my young friends—and I say it beseechingly, urgingly——

Always obey your parents, when they are present. This is the best policy in the long run, because if you don't they will make you. Most parents think they know better than you do, and you can generally make more by humoring that superstition than you can by acting on your own better judgment.

Be respectful to your superiors, if you have any, also to strangers, and sometimes to others. If a person offend you, and you are in doubt as to whether it was intentional or not, do not resort to extreme measures; simply watch your chance and hit him with a brick. That will be sufficient. If you shall find that he had not intended any offense, come out frankly and confess yourself in the wrong when you struck him; acknowledge it like a man and say you didn't mean to. Yes, always avoid violence; in this age of charity and kindliness, the time has gone by for such things. Leave dynamite to the low and unrefined.

Go to bed early, get up early—this is wise. Some authorities say get up with the sun; some others say get up with one thing, some with another. But a lark is really the best thing to get up with. It gives you a splendid reputation with everybody to know that you get up with the lark; and if you get the right kind of a lark, and work at him right, you can easily train him to get up at half past nine, every time—it is no trick at all.

Now as to the matter of lying. You want to be very careful about lying; otherwise you are nearly sure to get caught. Once caught, you can never again be, in the eyes of the good and the pure, what you were before. Many a young person has injured himself permanently through a single clumsy and ill-finished lie, the result of carelessness born of incomplete training. Some authorities hold that the young ought not to lie at all. That, of course, is putting it rather stronger than necessary; still, while I cannot go quite so far as that, I do maintain, and I believe I am right, that the young ought to be temperate in the use of this great art until practice and experience shall give them that confidence, elegance, and precision which alone can make the accomplishment graceful and profitable. Patience, diligence, painstaking attention to detail—these are the requirements; these, in time, will make the student perfect; upon these, and upon these only, may he rely as the sure foundation for future eminence. Think what tedious years of study, thought, practice, experience, went to the equipment of that peerless old master who was able to impose upon the whole world the lofty and sounding maxim that "truth is mighty and will prevail"—the most majestic compound fracture of fact which any of woman born has yet achieved. For the history of our race, and each individual's experience, are sown thick with evidence that a truth is not hard to kill and that a lie told well is immortal. There in

Boston is a monument of the man who discovered anæsthesia; many people are aware, in these latter days, that that man didn't discover it at all, but stole the discovery from another man. Is this truth mighty, and will it prevail? Ah no, my hearers, the monument is made of hardy material, but the lie it tells will outlast it a million years. An awkward, feeble, leaky lie is a thing which you ought to make it your unceasing study to avoid; such a lie as that has no more real permanence than an average truth. Why, you might as well tell the truth at once and be done with it. A feeble, stupid, preposterous lie will not live two years—except it be a slander upon somebody. It is indestructible, then, of course, but that is no merit of yours. A final word: begin your practice of this gracious and beautiful art early—begin now. If I had begun earlier, I could have learned how.

Never handle firearms carelessly. The sorrow and suffering that have been caused through the innocent but heedless handling of firearms by the young! Only four days ago, right in the next farmhouse to the one where I am spending the summer, a grandmother, old and gray and sweet, one of the loveliest spirits in the land, was sitting at her work, when her young grandson crept in and got down an old, battered, rusty gun which had not been touched for many years and was supposed not to be loaded, and pointed it at her, laughing and threatening to shoot. In her fright she ran screaming and pleading toward the door on the other side of the room; but as she passed him he placed the gun almost against her very breast and pulled the trigger! He had supposed it was not loaded. And he was right—it wasn't. So there wasn't any harm done. It is the only case of that kind I ever heard of. Therefore, just the same, don't you meddle with old unloaded firearms; they are the most deadly and unerring things that have ever been created by man. You don't have to take any pains at all with them; you don't have to have a rest, you don't have to have any sights on the gun, you don't have to take aim, even. No, you just pick out a relative and bang away, and you are sure to get him. A youth who can't hit a cathedral at thirty yards with a Gatling gun in three-quarters of an hour, can take up an old empty musket and bag his grandmother every time, at a hundred. Think what Waterloo would have been if one of the armies had been boys armed with old muskets supposed not to be loaded, and the other army had been composed of their female relations. The very thought of it makes one shudder.

There are many sorts of books; but good ones are the sort for the young to read. Remember that. They are a great, an inestimable, an unspeakable means of improvement. Therefore be careful in your selection, my young friends; be very careful; confine yourselves exclusively to Robertson's Sermons, Baxter's *Saint's Rest*, *The Innocents Abroad*, and works of that kind.

But I have said enough. I hope you will treasure up the instructions which I have given you, and make them a guide to your feet and a light to your understanding. Build your character thoughtfully and painstaking upon these precepts, and by and by, when you have got it built, you will be surprised and gratified to see how nicely and sharply it resembles everybody else's.

Mark Twain

The Traveller and His Dog

A Traveller, about to set out on his journey, saw his Dog stand at the door stretching himself. He asked him sharply: "What do you stand gaping there for? Everything is ready but you; so come with me instantly." The Dog, wagging his tail, replied: "O, master! I am quite ready; it is you for whom I am waiting."

The loiterer often imputes delay to his more active friend.

Aesop

from Tremendous Trifles

The whole object of travel is not to set foot on foreign lands; it is at last to set foot on one's own country as a foreign land.

G. K. Chesterton

from Leaves of Grass

There was a child went forth every day,
And the first object he looked upon and received with wonder, pity, love, or dread, that object he became,
And that object became part of him for the day, or a certain part of the day, or for many years, or stretching cycles of years.

The early lilacs became part of this child,
And grass, and white and red morning-glories, and white and red clover, and the song of the phœbe-bird,
And the Third Month lambs, and the sow's pink-faint litter, and the mare's foal, and the cow's calf,
And the noisy brood of the barn-yard, or by the mire of the pond-side,
And the fish suspending themselves so curiously below there — and the beautiful curious liquid,
And the water-plants with their graceful flat heads — all became part of him.

The field-sprouts of Fourth Month and Fifth
   Month became part of him,
Winter-grain sprouts, and those of the light-
   yellow corn, and the esculent roots of the
   garden,
And the apple-trees covered with blossoms, and
   the fruit afterward, and wood-berries, and the
   commonest weeds by the road;
And the old drunkard staggering home from
   the out-house of the tavern, whence he had
   lately risen,
And the school-mistress that passed on her way
   to the school,
And the friendly boys that passed — and the
   quarrel-some boys,
And the tidy and fresh-cheeked girls — and the
   barefoot boy and girl,
And all the changes of city and country,
   wherever he went.

His own parents,
He that had fathered him, and she that
   conceived him in her womb, and birthed him,
They gave this child more of themselves than
   that,

They gave him afterward every day — they and
of them became part of him.

The mother at home, quietly placing the dishes
on the supper-table,
The mother with mild words — clean her cap
and gown, a wholesome odor falling off her
person and clothes as she walks by;
The father, strong, self-sufficient, manly, mean,
angered, unjust,
The blow, the quick loud word, the tight
bargain, the crafty lure,
The family usages, the language, the company,
the furniture — the yearning and swelling
heart,
Affection that will not be gainsayed — the
sense of what is real — the thought if, after
all, it should prove unreal,
The doubts of day-time and the doubts of
night-time — the curious whether and how,
Whether that which appears so is so, or is it all
flashes and specks?
Men and women crowding fast in the streets —
if they are not flashes and specks, what are
they?

The streets themselves, and the façades of houses, and goods in the windows,
Vehicles, teams, the heavy-planked wharves — the huge crossing at the ferries,
The village on the highland, seen from afar at sunset — the river between,
Shadows, aureola and mist, light falling on roofs and gables of white or brown, three miles off,
The schooner near by, sleepily dropping down the tide — the little boat slack-towed astern,
The hurrying tumbling waves, quick-broken crests, slapping,
The strata of colored clouds, the long bar of maroon-tint, away solitary by itself — the spread of purity it lies motionless in,
The horizon's edge, the flying sea-crow, the fragrance of salt-marsh and shore-mud;
These became part of that child who went forth every day, and who now goes, and will always go forth every day,
And these become part of him or her that peruses them here.

Walt Whitman

from A Plea for Captain John Brown

the one great rule of composition — and if I were a professor of rhetoric I should insist on this — is, to *speak the truth*.

Henry David Thoreau

from The Living Thoughts of Voltaire
by André Maurois

Tolerance: What is tolerance?—it is the consequence of humanity. We are all formed of frailty and error; let us pardon reciprocally each other's folly—that is the first law of nature.

Voltaire

The Crow and the Pitcher

A Crow perishing with thirst saw a pitcher, and, hoping to find water, flew to it with great delight. When he reached it, he discovered to his grief that it contained so little water that he could not possibly get at it. He tried everything he could think of to reach the water, but all his efforts were in vain. At last he collected as many stones as he could carry, and dropped them one by one with his beak into the pitcher, until he brought the water within his reach, and thus saved his life.

Necessity is the mother of invention.

Aesop

Try, Try Again

'Tis a lesson you should heed,
    Try, try again;
If at first you don't succeed,
    Try, try again;
Then your courage should appear,
For, if you will persevere,
You will conquer, never fear;
    Try, try again.

Once or twice though you should fail,
    Try, try again;
If you would at last prevail,
    Try, try again;
If we strive, 'tis no disgrace
Though we do not win the race;
What should you do in the case?
    Try, try again.

If you find your task is hard,
    Try, try again;
Time will bring you your reward,
    Try, try again.

All that other folks can do,
Why, with patience, should not you?
Only keep this rule in view:
    Try, try again.

T. H. Palmer

from The Life of Samuel Johnson

I regretted that I had lost much of my disposition to admire, which people generally do as they advance in life.

Johnson. "Sir, as a man advances in life, he gets what is better than admiration,—judgment, to estimate things at their true value."

James Boswell

Desiderata

Go placidly amid the noise and the haste,
and remember what peace there may be in silence.
As far as possible, without surrender,
be on good terms with all persons.
Speak your truth quietly and clearly;
and listen to others, even to the dull and the ignorant;
they too have their story.
Avoid loud and aggressive persons;
they are vexatious to the spirit.

If you compare yourself with others,
you may become vain or bitter,
for always there will be greater and lesser persons than yourself.
Enjoy your achievements as well as your plans.
Keep interested in your own career, however humble;
it is a real possession in the changing fortunes of time.

Exercise caution in your business affairs,
for the world is full of trickery.
But let this not blind you to what virtue
  there is;
many persons strive for high ideals,
and everywhere life is full of heroism.

Be yourself. Especially do not feign affection.
Neither be cynical about love;
for in the face of all aridity and
  disenchantment,
it is as perennial as the grass.
Take kindly the counsel of the years,
gracefully surrendering the things of youth.

Nurture strength of spirit to shield you in
  sudden misfortune.
But do not distress yourself with dark
  imaginings.
Many fears are born of fatigue and loneliness.

Beyond a wholesome discipline, be gentle with
  yourself.

You are a child of the universe no less than the
 trees and the stars;
you have a right to be here.
And whether or not it is clear to you,
no doubt the universe is unfolding as it should.

Therefore be at peace with God,
whatever you conceive Him to be.
And whatever your labors and aspirations,
in the noisy confusion of life, keep peace in
 your soul.
With all its sham, drudgery and broken dreams,
it is still a beautiful world.
Be cheerful. Strive to be happy.

Max Ehrmann

from Mark Twain's Notebook

If you tell the truth you don't have to remember anything.

Mark Twain

Three Questions

It once occurred to a certain king, that if he always knew the right time to begin everything; if he knew who were the right people to listen to, and whom to avoid; and, above all, if he always knew what was the most important thing to do, he would never fail in anything he might undertake.

And this thought having occurred to him, he had it proclaimed throughout his kingdom that he would give a great reward to any one who would teach him what was the right time for every action, and who were the most necessary people, and how he might know what was the most important thing to do.

And learned men came to the King, but they all answered his questions differently.

In reply to the first question, some said that to know the right time for every action, one must draw up in advance, a table of days, months and years, and must live strictly according to it. Only thus, said they, could everything be done at its proper time. Others declared that it was impossible to decide beforehand the right time for every action; but that, not letting oneself be absorbed in idle pastimes, one should always attend to all that was going on, and then do what was most needful. Others, again, said that however attentive the King might be to what was going on, it was impossible for one man to decide correctly the right time for every action, but that he should have a Council of wise men, who would help him to fix the proper time for everything.

But then again others said there were some things which could not wait to be laid before a Council, but about which one had at once to decide whether to undertake them or not. But in order to decide that, one must know beforehand what was going to happen. It is only magicians who know that; and, therefore, in order to know the right time for every action, one must consult magicians.

Equally various were the answers to the second question. Some said, the people the King most needed were his councillors; others, the priests; others, the doctors; while some said the warriors were the most necessary.

To the third question, as to what was the most

important occupation: some replied that the most important thing in the world was science. Others said it was skill in warfare; and others, again, that it was religious worship.

All the answers being different, the King agreed with none of them, and gave the reward to none. But still wishing to find the right answers to his questions, he decided to consult a hermit, widely renowned for his wisdom.

The hermit lived in a wood which he never quitted, and he received none but common folk. So the King put on simple clothes, and before reaching the hermit's cell dismounted from his horse, and, leaving his body-guard behind, went on alone.

When the King approached, the hermit was digging the ground in front of his hut. Seeing the King, he greeted him and went on digging. The hermit was frail and weak, and each time he stuck his spade into the ground and turned a little earth, he breathed heavily.

The King went up to him and said: "I have come to you, wise hermit, to ask you to answer three questions: How can I learn to do the right thing at the right time? Who are the people I most need, and to whom should I, therefore, pay more attention than to the rest? And, what affairs are the most important, and need my first attention?"

The hermit listened to the King, but answered nothing. He just spat on his hand and recommenced digging.

"You are tired," said the King, "let me take the spade and work awhile for you."

"Thanks!" said the hermit, and, giving the spade to the King, he sat down on the ground.

When he had dug two beds, the King stopped and repeated his questions. The hermit again gave no answer, but rose, stretched out his hand for the spade, and said:

"Now rest awhile—and let me work a bit."

But the King did not give him the spade, and continued to dig. One hour passed, and another. The sun began to sink behind the trees, and the King at last stuck the spade into the ground, and said:

"I came to you, wise man, for an answer to my questions. If you can give me none, tell me so, and I will return home."

"Here comes some one running," said the hermit, "let us see who it is."

The King turned round, and saw a bearded man come running out of the wood. The man held his hands pressed against his stomach, and blood was flowing from under them. When he reached the King, he fell fainting on the ground moaning feebly. The King and the hermit unfastened the man's clothing. There was a large wound in his stomach. The King washed it as best he could, and bandaged it with his handkerchief and with a towel the hermit had. But the blood would not stop flowing, and the King again and again removed the bandage soaked with warm blood, and washed and rebandaged the wound. When at last the blood ceased flowing, the man revived and asked for something to drink. The King brought fresh water and gave it to him. Meanwhile the sun had set, and it had become cool. So the King, with the hermit's help, carried the wounded man into the hut and laid him on the bed. Lying on the bed the man closed his eyes and was quiet; but the King was so tired with his walk and with the work he had done, that he crouched down on the threshold, and also fell asleep — so soundly that he slept all through the short summer night. When he awoke in the morning, it was long before he could remember where he was, or who was the strange bearded man lying on the bed and gazing intently at him with shining eyes.

"Forgive me!" said the bearded man in a weak voice, when he saw that the King was awake and was looking at him.

"I do not know you, and have nothing to forgive you for," said the King.

"You do not know me, but I know you. I am that enemy of yours who swore to revenge himself on you, because you executed his brother and seized his property. I knew you had gone alone to see the hermit, and I resolved to kill you on your way back. But the day passed and you did not return. So I came out from my ambush to find you, and I came upon your bodyguard, and they recognized me, and wounded me. I escaped from them, but should have bled to death had you not dressed my wound. I wished to kill you, and you have saved my life. Now, if I live, and if you wish it, I will serve you as your most faithful slave, and will bid my sons do the same. Forgive me!"

The King was very glad to have made peace with his enemy so easily, and to have gained him for a friend, and he not only forgave him, but said he would send his servants and his own physician to attend him, and promised to restore his property.

Having taken leave of the wounded man, the King went out into the porch and looked around for the hermit. Before going away he wished once more to beg an answer to the questions he had put. The hermit was outside, on his knees, sowing seeds in the beds that had been dug the day before.

The King approached him, and said:

"For the last time, I pray you to answer my questions, wise man."

"You have already been answered!" said the hermit, still crouching on his thin legs, and looking up at the King, who stood before him.

"How answered? What do you mean?" asked the King.

"Do you not see," replied the hermit. "If you had not pitied my weakness yesterday, and had not dug those beds for me, but had gone your way, that man would have attacked you, and you would have repented of not having stayed with me. So the most important time was when you were digging the beds; and I was the most important man; and to do me good was your most important business. Afterwards when that man ran to us, the most important time was when you were attending to him, for if you had not bound up his wounds he would have died without having made peace with you. So he was the most important man, and what you did for him was your most important business. Remember then: there is only one time that is important — Now! It is the most important time because it is the only time when we have any power. The most necessary man is he with whom you are, for no man knows whether he will ever have dealings with any one else: and the most important affair is, to do him good, because for that purpose alone was man sent into this life!"

Leo Tolstoy

Index of Poets and Authors

Aesop 24, 120, 128
Allen, E. A. 5
Allen, James 50
Aurelius, Marcus 37, 68
Austen, Jane 90

Boswell, James 131
Brontë, Charlotte 99

Chesterton, G. K. 121
Cicero, Marcus Tullius 11

Dickens, Charles 16
Dickinson, Emily 3, 31, 85

Ehrmann, Max 132
Eliot, George 55, 86
Emerson, Ralph Waldo 91
Epictetus 57
Epicurus 88

Ferguson, S. C. 5
Fern, Fanny 69
Fitzgerald, F. Scott 62
Frost, Robert 21

Gibran, Kahlil 25, 53
Goldman, Emma 83

Hemingway, Ernest   30
Henley, William Ernest   46
Hugo, Victor   4

Johnson, Georgia Douglas   113

King, Martin Luther   6
Kipling, Rudyard   33

La Bruyère, Jean de   29
La Fontaine, Jean de   8
Longfellow, Henry Wadsworth   101

Malloch, Douglas   27
Maitland, Ella Fuller   72
Melville, Herman   14
Montaigne, Michel de   36, 49

Palmer, T. H.   129
Petrarch   64
Poe, Edgar Allan   81

Richards, Laura E.   74
Roosevelt, Theodore   43
Rossetti, Christina   13

Seneca, Lucius Annaeus   95
Shakespeare, William   7, 15
Stowe, Harriet Beecher   17

Teasdale, Sara   82
Thoreau, Henry David   23, 59, 126

Tolstoy, Leo 10, 32, 56, 84, 136
Twain, Mark 114, 135

Van Dyke, Henry 42, 103
Voltaire 127

Warner, Charles Dudley 100
Washington, Booker T. 38
Whitman, Walt 73, 122
Wilcox, Ella Wheeler 12, 66
Wordsworth, William 97

Permissions Acknowledgements

Extract from 'A New Sense of Direction' reprinted by arrangement with The Heirs to the Estate of Martin Luther King Jr., c/o Writers House as agent for the proprietor New York, NY. Copyright © 1967 by Dr Martin Luther King, Jr. Renewed © 1995 by Coretta Scott King.

'The Hare and the Tortoise' from *The Complete Fables of Jean de la Fontaine*, translated by Norman B. Spector © 1988 by Northwestern University Press. All rights reserved.

'Your World' by Georgia Douglas Johnson from *Shadowed Dreams: Women's Poetry of the Harlem Renaissance* ed. Maureen Honey (2006) published with permission from the Copyright Clearance Centre on behalf of Rutgers University Press.

MACMILLAN COLLECTOR'S LIBRARY

Own the world's great works of literature in one beautiful collectible library

Designed and curated to appeal to book lovers everywhere, Macmillan Collector's Library editions are small enough to travel with you and striking enough to take pride of place on your bookshelf. These much-loved literary classics also make the perfect gift.

Beautifully made, every Macmillan Collector's Library book adheres to the same high production values. Each hardback features gilt edges, a ribbon marker and cloth binding, and every paperback has a bespoke illustrated cover.

Discover a new and exciting anthology or cherish your favourite classic stories with this elegant collection.

Macmillan Collector's Library: own, collect, and treasure

Discover the full range at
panmacmillan.com/mcl